3800 17 0069124 3
HIGH LIFE HIGHLAND

D0987876

THE ADVENTURES OF
ROBIN HOOD

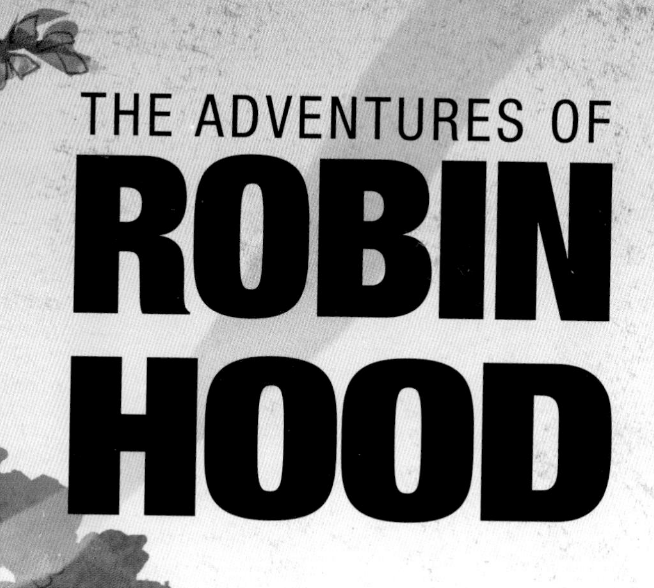

Retold by Russell Punter

Illustrated by Matteo Pincelli

Series editors:
Lesley Sims and Jane Chisholm

Consultant: Mike Collins

The world of Robin Hood
River Poulter
River Meden
River Maun
Marshes
DERBY SHIRE
Outlaws' encampment
Rainworth Water
Robin first meets Little John here
Sherwood Forest
River where Robin first meets Friar Tuck
River Leen
Locksley Hall
Alan-a-Dale's cottage
Guy of Gisbourne's Manor House
Nottingham Castle
Nottingham

LINCOLN
SHIRE
NOTTINGHAM
SHIRE
River Greet
Arlingford Castle
River Trent
Dover Beck
SCOTLAND
IRELAND
Nottingham
ENGLAND
WALES
Scale
0
10 km
6 miles

England, 1194
With King Richard I away fighting wars in the Holy Land of the Eastern Mediterranean, the country is under the control of his power-hungry brother, Prince John.
Under orders from the Prince, the crooked Sheriff of Nottingham regularly storms through local towns and villages, demanding money from those who can least afford it.
And today is no exception...
GATHER AROUND, PEASANTS!
LISTEN TO THE SHERIFF!

WE'RE HERE TO COLLECT YOUR TAXES.
PAY UP, OR YOU'LL SUFFER THE CONSEQUENCES!

WE GAVE ALL WE HAD LAST TIME!
WE'RE JUST POOR, WORKING FOLK.
HAVE PITY ON US, MY LORD!
HOW DARE YOU DEFY AN OFFICER OF PRINCE JOHN! PAY UP OR MY MEN WILL BURN THIS VILLAGE TO THE GROUND.

THE VILLAGERS HAVE NO CHOICE...

WHEN THE SHERIFF AND HIS MEN HAVE FINISHED...
JUST ONE MORE VILLAGE TO VISIT TODAY, MY LORD!
YOU PROCEED. I HAVE BUSINESS BACK IN NOTTINGHAM.
THE TAX COLLECTORS MAKE THEIR WAY THROUGH SHERWOOD FOREST...
HA HA! DID YOU SEE THOSE VILLAGERS SQUIRM?
OUR TREASURE CHEST IS ALMOST FULL!
SUDDENLY...
THWACK!

IT'S AN AMBUSH!
GOOD DAY, GENTLEMEN. I SEE YOU'VE BEEN BUSY, AS USUAL.
STAND ASIDE IN THE NAME OF THE SHERIFF, YOU THIEVES!
IT'S THE SHERIFF WHO'S THE THIEF – STEALING FROM THE POOR, SO HE CAN LIVE IN LUXURY.
HAND OVER YOUR TREASURE CHEST!

YOU'LL **PAY** FOR THIS, YOU **GREEDY KNAVES!**
WE HAVE **NO NEED** OF YOUR **LOOT**.
BUT WE'LL **RETURN** THE MONEY TO THOSE WHO **NEED** IT.
MINUTES LATER...
I WISH YOU A **GOOD JOURNEY.** YOUR HORSES SHOULD FIND THEIR WAY HOME – **EVENTUALLY.**
YOU **ROGUE!** WHO **ARE** YOU?
'ROBIN HOOD' IS AS GOOD A NAME AS ANY. **FAREWELL**, GENTLEMEN!

OVER THE WEEKS THAT FOLLOW, THE MYSTERIOUS 'ROBIN HOOD' STRIKES TIME AFTER TIME....
SOON THE SHERIFF OF NOTTINGHAM IS AT HIS WITS' END...
THIS ROBIN HOOD IS MAKING A FOOL OF ME! I WANT HIM FOUND AND KILLED.
I'VE HEARD THAT A LOCAL MILLER HAS HAD DEALINGS WITH HIM.
THEN LET US ACT!

SO THAT AFTERNOON, ON THE OUTSKIRTS OF SHERWOOD FOREST...
YOU THERE, MILLER! I HEAR YOU KNOW THE OUTLAW ROBIN HOOD?
WE ALL KNOW OF ROBIN HOOD IN THESE PARTS. BUT HE'S NO OUTLAW.
HA! WHAT ELSE DO YOU CALL A ROGUE WHO ROBS LOYAL SUBJECTS?
HE GIVES IT ALL TO THE POOR. AND HE ONLY TAKES FROM THOSE WHO CAN AFFORD IT.
YES, SON, FROM RICH MEN LIKE PRINCE JOHN'S TAX COLLECTORS.

I'M LOYAL TO ROBIN HOOD, AND THE TRUE RULER OF ENGLAND, HIS MAJESTY KING RICHARD.
HOW DARE YOU SHOW DISLOYALTY TO YOUR RULER!
SWEAR LOYALTY TO PRINCE JOHN OR YOU'LL PAY WITH YOUR LIFE!
NEVER!
SO BE IT!
FATHER!
CLASH!

AAAAAGH!
YOU DOGS!
LET THIS BE A LESSON TO ALL THOSE WHO SIDE WITH OUTLAWS LIKE ROBIN HOOD.
TAKE COURAGE, LAD. I KNOW SOMEONE WHO'LL GLADLY TAKE CARE OF YOU.
THANK YOU, WILL.

AS THE SHERIFF RIDES OFF...
MY LORD!
MY NAME'S WURMAN. IF YOU SEEK ROBIN HOOD, MY MASTER, ROBERT OF LOCKSLEY, MIGHT KNOW WHERE HE IS.
MY MASTER OFTEN SPEAKS HIGHLY OF ROBIN HOOD AND HIS FIGHT AGAINST THE PRINCE.
HOW MIGHT I GET CLOSE TO LOCKSLEY?
TOMORROW HE IS TO BE WED TO LADY MARIAN, DAUGHTER OF LORD FITZWALTER.
LOCKSLEY HALL IS OPEN TO ALL TONIGHT FOR THE WEDDING FEAST.
YOU HAVE DONE WELL.

ON HIS WAY BACK TO NOTTINGHAM, THE SHERIFF CALLS ON HIS ALLY, GUY OF GISBOURNE...
SO YOU WISH ME TO SPY ON LOCKSLEY?
WURMAN WILL AID YOU. FIND OUT WHAT LOCKSLEY KNOWS OF ROBIN HOOD...
...AND YOU'LL BE RICHLY REWARDED.
AND SO, THAT NIGHT AT LOCKSLEY HALL...
HERE'S GOOD FORTUNE TO ROBERT AND MARIAN!
AND MISFORTUNE TO THAT IMPOSTER PRINCE JOHN!
HA HA!

LATER THAT EVENING...
LOCKSLEY DOESN'T DESERVE A BRIDE AS BEAUTIFUL AS LADY MARIAN.
IS IT NOT AS I TOLD THE SHERIFF, MY LORD?
LOCKSLEY'S NO LOYAL SERVANT OF THE PRINCE, THAT MUCH IS CLEAR.
BUT I NEED MORE PROOF OF HIS TIES WITH ROBIN HOOD.
MOMENTS LATER...
COME ALONG, MUCH.
I THINK I SEE THE PROOF YOU NEED, MY LORD. THAT MAN, WILLIAM SCATHELOCKE, BRINGS WITH HIM THE MILLER'S SON, MUCH MIDDLETON.
YOU WOULD DO WELL TO FOLLOW THEM.

AND SO...

YOU WILL BE SAFE HERE, LAD. **ROBIN HOOD** HIMSELF WILL LOOK AFTER YOU.

SO, LOCKSLEY **IS** IN LEAGUE WITH ROBIN HOOD.

I'LL SEE TO IT THAT LOCKSLEY'S WEDDING DAY IS A **MEMORABLE ONE.**

AND WITH HIM OUT OF THE WAY, MARIAN CAN BE **MINE!**

THE NEXT DAY, ROBERT AND MARIAN'S WEDDING CEREMONY IS ABOUT TO BEGIN...
WHEN SUDDENLY...
STOP THE WEDDING! THIS MAN IS A TRAITOR TO PRINCE JOHN!
WHO ARE YOU TO CALL ME A TRAITOR IN MY OWN CHAPEL?

I AM GUY OF GISBOURNE, HERE TO DO THE PRINCE'S BIDDING. DO YOU DENY YOUR TREACHERY?
I AM A LOYAL SERVANT OF RICHARD, OUR RIGHTFUL KING, AND I'M NO TRAITOR.
THEN WHY DO YOU CONSORT WITH THE OUTLAW ROBIN HOOD?
I DO NOT.
LIAR!
I DO NOT CONSORT WITH ROBIN HOOD... BECAUSE I AM ROBIN HOOD!

SEIZE HIM!
I'LL BE BACK FOR YOU, MARIAN.
WITH A NOD TO WILLIAM, ROBERT MAKES HIS ESCAPE...
CRASH!

OOF!
WILLIAM LOSES NO TIME...
THIS SHOULD HOLD GISBOURNE AND HIS THUGS FOR A WHILE.
INSIDE...
THUD!
THUMP!
GET THESE DOORS OPEN, YOU FOOLS!
THUD!

ROBERT AND WILLIAM LEAVE THE LOCKSLEY ESTATE BEHIND...
...TO START A NEW LIFE AS ROBIN HOOD AND WILL SCARLET IN SHERWOOD FOREST.
WHEN THEY HAVE SET UP CAMP, ROBIN SENDS WILL TO COLLECT MUCH. IT'S NOT LONG BEFORE THE TRIO ARE JOINED BY MORE RECRUITS...
PRINCE JOHN AND THE SHERIFF HAVE LEFT US WITH NOTHING!
ALL ARE WELCOME HERE. BUT YOU MUST LEARN THE WAYS OF THE FOREST.

ROBIN PASSES ON THE SKILLS LEARNED FROM THE FORESTERS ON HIS ESTATE...
GATHERING FOOD...
THESE **BLACK** BERRIES ARE **GOOD**, BUT THE **RED** ONES ARE **POISONOUS**.
TRACKING ANIMALS...
THESE DEER PRINTS ARE **FRESH**.
AND USING CAMOUFLAGE...
THE **TREES** ARE OUR GREATEST ALLY WHEN IT COMES TO **DISGUISE**.
ROBIN?
HA HA!

ONE DAY, ROBIN IS ON THE OUTSKIRTS OF SHERWOOD, WHEN...
HELLO STRANGER! WHAT BUSINESS DO YOU HAVE IN THE FOREST?
LET ME PASS AND I MAY TELL YOU.

I WAS HERE FIRST. MOVE BACK!
YOU'RE MISTAKEN, FRIEND. STAND ASIDE OR PREPARE FOR A DUCKING!
I FANCY IT'S YOU WHO'S DUE A BATH.

WHACK!
CRACK!
WOOOAH!
HA HA HAAA!
SPLASH!

HA HA! IT SEEMS I MUST GIVE WAY ON THIS OCCASION. MIGHT I KNOW MY WORTHY OPPONENT'S **NAME?**
I'M **JOHN LITTLE.**

NEVER WAS A NAME **LESS** SUITED! WHAT BRINGS YOU TO THE FOREST?
MY LANDS HAVE BEEN TAKEN BY PRINCE JOHN'S TAX COLLECTORS. I PLAN TO JOIN ROBIN HOOD, IF HE'LL TAKE ME.

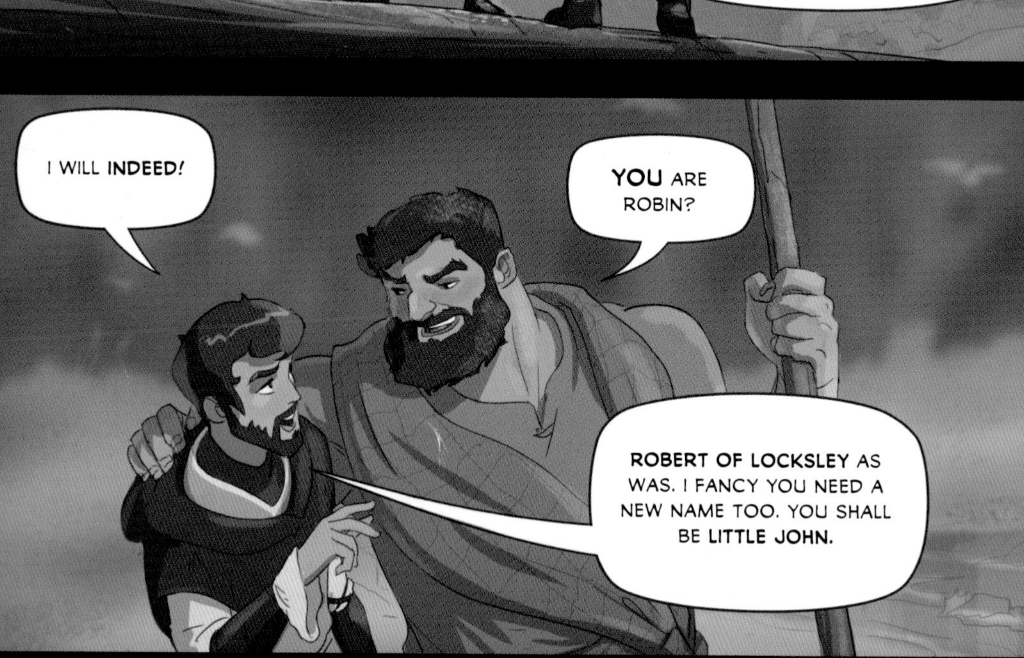
I WILL **INDEED!**
YOU ARE ROBIN?
ROBERT OF LOCKSLEY AS WAS. I FANCY YOU NEED A NEW NAME TOO. YOU SHALL BE **LITTLE JOHN.**

LITTLE JOHN SOON BECOMES A USEFUL ADDITION TO ROBIN'S BAND, PASSING ON HIS FIGHTING SKILLS...
HOLD THE STAFF HIGHER, LAD!
THWACK!
KEEP THE BOW UP 'TIL THE ARROW IS WELL AWAY.
A BEAR COULDN'T GET OUT OF THIS HOLD!
GNNNFFF!
BLOCK A BLOW TO THE CHEST LIKE THIS!
CLUNK!

THANKS TO LITTLE JOHN, THE OUTLAWS ARE SOON READY TO FIGHT...
WHAT WE NEED NOW IS SOMEONE TO CARE FOR OUR **SOULS.**
I'VE HEARD TALK OF A **MONK** WHO WORKS AS A **FERRYMAN** BY THE RIVER.
A **STRANGE** OCCUPATION FOR A **MONK?**
THEY SAY HE **FELL OUT** WITH THE ABBOT OF HIS MONASTERY OVER THE PRINCE'S **HIGH TAXES.**
HE SOUNDS LIKE A **FELLOW REBEL.**
SO ROBIN PAYS A VISIT TO THE MONK...
I'LL DISCOVER THIS HOLY MAN'S **COURAGE** BY TESTING HIS **PATIENCE.**

GOOD DAY, FATHER! I WISH TO CROSS THE RIVER.
I SHALL BE WITH YOU PRESENTLY, MY SON.

THE MONK ROWS OVER TO ROBIN...
AND FERRIES HIM ACROSS THE RIVER.

BUT THEN...
I'VE CHANGED MY MIND. PLEASE ROW ME BACK.

AND SO...
SIGH.

BUT THEN...
I'VE CHANGED MY MIND AGAIN. I SHALL CROSS AFTER ALL!

THIS KNAVE IS HAVING FUN WITH ME. WELL TWO CAN PLAY AT THAT GAME...

THERE'S ANOTHER WAY TO CROSS, MY SON...
WOOAAAH!

FORGIVE ME, LORD.
SPLASH!

I WOULD HAVE YOU JOIN ME, FATHER!

WAAAAH!
SPLOSH!
MY WORD!
HA HA!
THE PAIR REACH THE BANK, AND AFTER ROBIN INTRODUCES HIMSELF...
MY NAME IS TUCK. I CONFESS I HAD THOUGHTS OF JOINING YOUR BAND.
BUT I WAS AFRAID YOU MIGHT NOT HAVE ENOUGH PROVISIONS FOR SOMEONE WITH MY, ERM, APPETITE.
THE FOREST PROVIDES US WITH GAME AND BERRIES. AND OUR FRIENDS OUTSIDE SUPPLY US WITH BEEF, PORK, WINE AND...
WHEN DO I START?

SOON ROBIN AND HIS MEN CONTROL THE FOREST...
THE POOR ARE GIVEN COINS AND ALLOWED TO PASS THROUGH UNHINDERED.
WHILE THE RICH ARE 'INVITED' TO EAT WITH THE OUTLAWS...
...AND TO PAY FOR THE MEAL WITH HALF THEIR MONEY.
ONE MORNING, THE LATEST VISITOR TO THE FOREST IS BROUGHT BEFORE ROBIN...
WE CAUGHT THIS **LAD** SNEAKING UP TO THE CAMP.
HE PUT UP QUITE A **FIGHT.**

MARIAN!
I CAME TO BRING YOU NEWS OF YOUR ESTATE.
PRINCE JOHN HAS GIVEN LOCKSLEY HALL AND ALL YOUR LAND TO GUY OF GISBOURNE.
HOW DARE HE!
WORSE STILL, GUY HAS MADE IT CLEAR HE INTENDS TO MAKE ME HIS WIFE.
THE FIEND! I SHALL CONFRONT HIM.
YOU WOULDN'T STAND A CHANCE.
WE MUST WAIT UNTIL HE COMES TO US.

I MUST RETURN TO MY FATHER BEFORE I'M MISSED.
WHEN MY LANDS ARE RESTORED, WE'LL COMPLETE OUR MARRIAGE CEREMONY.
AS MARIAN HEADS HOME...
I MUST STOP GISBOURNE FROM GETTING HIS HANDS ON MY FAMILY TREASURE.
YOU'D BE RECOGNIZED, ROBIN. I SHALL GO WITH MUCH.
LATER THAT DAY, WILL AND MUCH ARRIVE AT LOCKSLEY HALL...
THE PLACE IS SWARMING WITH THE SHERIFF'S MEN!
WAIT HERE WHILE I SNEAK INSIDE.

MINUTES LATER, WILL EMERGES...
STOP THAT MAN!
RUN, MUCH!
NO TIME FOR US TO GET CLEAR...
IN HERE, QUICK!
TAKE THIS AND GIVE IT TO ROBIN!
WHAT ABOUT YOU?
SSSH!
GOT YOU!

SOON WILL IS SURROUNDED...
THE GAME'S UP, SCATHELOCKE, OR WHATEVER YOU CALL YOURSELF NOW.
YOU DON'T SCARE ME!
WE'LL SEE HOW BRAVE YOU ARE WHEN YOU'RE HANGING FROM A NOOSE OUTSIDE NOTTINGHAM CASTLE!
TAKE HIM!
WHEN THE COAST IS CLEAR...
I MUST TELL ROBIN WHAT'S HAPPENED.
BACK IN THE FOREST...
WE HAVE TO RESCUE WILL BEFORE IT'S TOO LATE.

YES, BUT WE'LL NEVER FIGHT OUR WAY PAST THE GUARDS.
THEN WE SHALL HAVE TO USE CUNNING.
WILL ASKED ME TO GIVE YOU THIS.
SO WILL WAS ABLE TO GET SOME OF THE LOCKSLEY TREASURE! BUT I'D GLADLY GIVE IT ALL TO HAVE HIM BACK.
THE NEXT MORNING, ROBIN AND HIS MEN REACH NOTTINGHAM.
THIS IS WHERE WE SPLIT UP. YOU ALL KNOW WHAT TO DO.

OUTSIDE THE CASTLE, WILL IS BROUGHT TO THE SCAFFOLD...
HERE COMES ROBIN HOOD'S FRIEND!
THE POOR SOUL.
THE SHERIFF AND HIS MEN SHOULD BE ASHAMED.
IF ONLY ROBIN HOOD WERE HERE.
MAKE WAY FOR AN OLD MAN!

WHERE IS LUKE LONGSHANK, THE HANGMAN?
I DON'T KNOW, SHERIFF.
FOOL! HOW CAN WE PROCEED WITHOUT HIM?

IF I MIGHT BE OF SERVICE, MY LORD...?
WHO ARE YOU?

I WAS ONCE A HANGMAN TO KING HENRY. I TAUGHT LONGSHANK ALL HE KNOWS.

THEN LET US WASTE NO MORE TIME. STRING UP THE PRISONER!

SEE HOW WE DEAL WITH THE **ALLIES** OF **ROBIN HOOD!**

BUT THEN...
AND SEE HOW **ROBIN HOOD** IS **TRUE** TO HIS **FRIENDS!**
WHAT?

THE REST OF THE OUTLAWS SPRING INTO ACTION...
FIRE AWAY, LADS!
HELP!
UURGH!
AAGH!

THEY'RE GETTING AWAY, YOU FOOLS! AFTER THEM!

MEANWHILE, AT A NEARBY INN...
ANOTHER FLAGON OF ALE, MASTER LONGSHANK?
HIC! BLESS YOU FATHER!

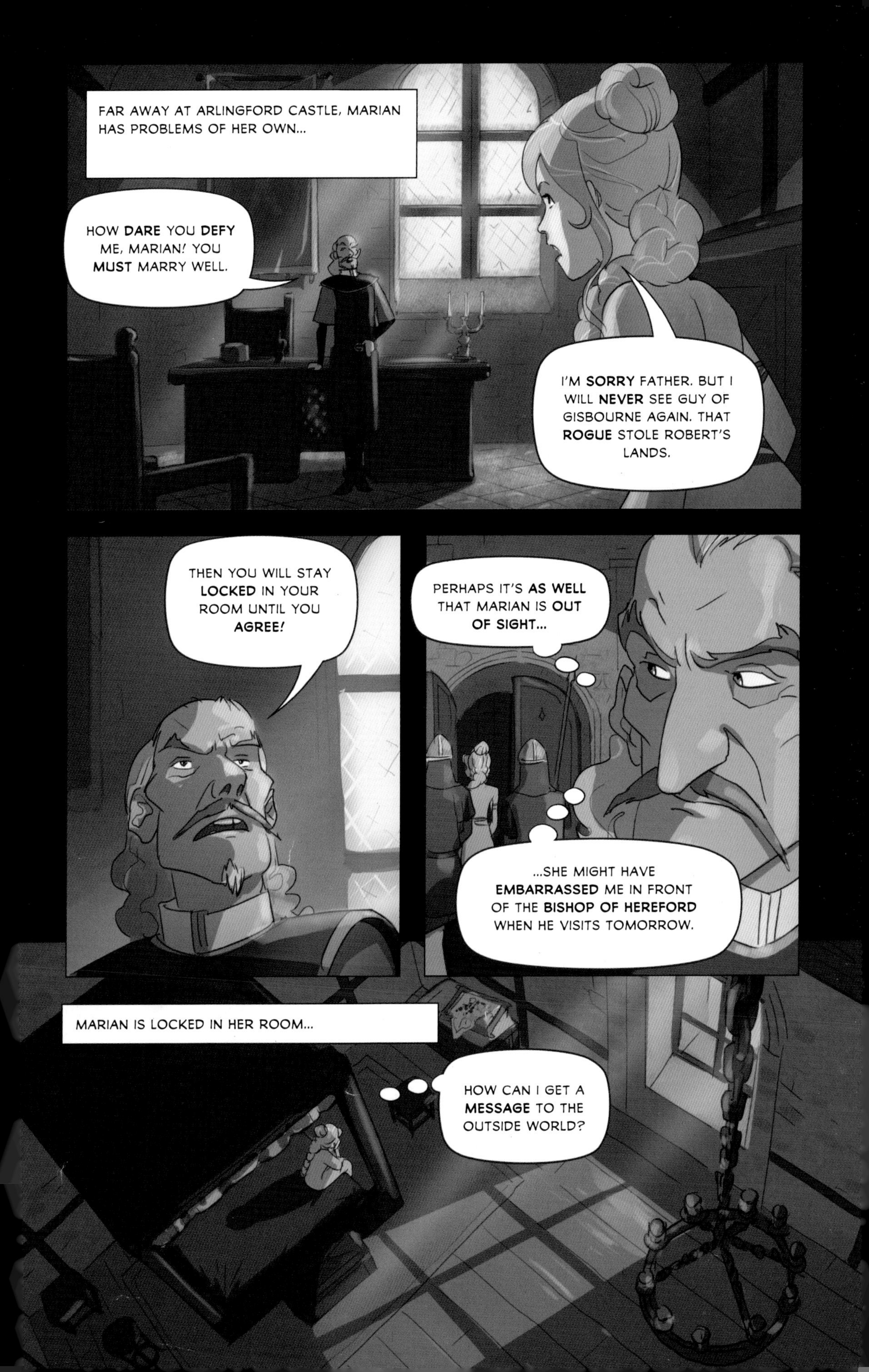
FAR AWAY AT ARLINGFORD CASTLE, MARIAN HAS PROBLEMS OF HER OWN...
HOW DARE YOU DEFY ME, MARIAN! YOU MUST MARRY WELL.
I'M SORRY FATHER. BUT I WILL NEVER SEE GUY OF GISBOURNE AGAIN. THAT ROGUE STOLE ROBERT'S LANDS.
THEN YOU WILL STAY LOCKED IN YOUR ROOM UNTIL YOU AGREE!
PERHAPS IT'S AS WELL THAT MARIAN IS OUT OF SIGHT...
...SHE MIGHT HAVE EMBARRASSED ME IN FRONT OF THE BISHOP OF HEREFORD WHEN HE VISITS TOMORROW.
MARIAN IS LOCKED IN HER ROOM...
HOW CAN I GET A MESSAGE TO THE OUTSIDE WORLD?

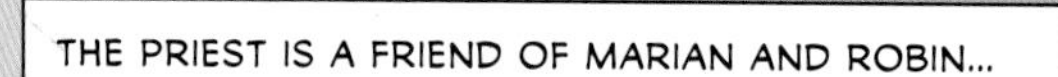

HE PAYS A VISIT TO ROBIN...

IT SEEMS MARIAN IS A PRISONER AT ARLINGFORD.

HOW CAN WE RESCUE HER?

THE PRIEST TOLD ME THAT THE BISHOP OF HEREFORD IS DUE TO VISIT MARIAN'S FATHER TOMORROW.
WHAT OF IT?
I'LL WAGER NO ONE AT ARLINGFORD CASTLE WILL HAVE MET THE BISHOP BEFORE.
I THINK I SEE YOUR PLAN...
THE NEXT EVENING, AS THE BISHOP'S PARTY ARE ON THEIR WAY TO ARLINGFORD...
HOLD THERE!
WHAT IS THE MEANING OF THIS?
AN INVITATION TO DINE WITH US, MY LORD. WE TRUST YOU'LL NOT REFUSE.
SOON AFTER...
MY LORD BISHOP. WELCOME TO ARLINGFORD CASTLE.

MARIAN'S FATHER TREATS HIS GUEST TO A FINE DINNER...
THANK YOU FOR YOUR HOSPITALITY, LORD FITZWALTER. IT'S A PITY YOUR DAUGHTER WASN'T ABLE TO JOIN US.
AS I SAY, MY LORD, SHE IS CONFINED IN HER ROOM UNTIL SHE LEARNS TO OBEY HER FATHER.
PERHAPS I COULD MAKE HER SEE SENSE?
I WOULD BE MOST GRATEFUL, MY LORD.
AND SO...
LISTEN TO THE BISHOP, MARIAN.
IF WE MIGHT BE ALONE, LORD FITZWALTER?

TUCK AND MARIAN REACH THE GATEHOUSE...

THE PORTCULLIS IS **DOWN,** AND THE MECHANISM FOR OPENING IT LIES IN THE GATEHOUSE.

YOU THERE, GATEKEEPER. **OPEN UP THIS GATE!**

ONLY **LORD FITZWALTER** MAY ORDER IT OPEN AT THIS HOUR.

HOW DARE YOU! BOW DOWN BEFORE A BISHOP!

FORGIVE ME, LORD!
BOP!
OOF!

MARIAN RAISES THE PORTCULLIS AND THE PAIR MAKE THEIR ESCAPE...
TO SHERWOOD!

AND SOON...
WE SHALL NEVER BE PARTED AGAIN.

WEEKS PASS WITHOUT INCIDENT, UNTIL ONE DAY...
LOOK, ROBIN!
Nottingham Goose Fair
Archery Contest
- open to all
A silver arrow to
the best bowman
HMM. I COULD USE A CHALLENGE.

YOU CAN'T BE SERIOUS! THE SHERIFF HIMSELF IS TO JUDGE THE CONTEST.
YOU'D BE ARRESTED ON SIGHT!
I CAN'T MISS THIS CHANCE TO TAKE A PRIZE FROM THE SHERIFF. I'LL DISGUISE MYSELF AS AN OLD CRUSADER, BACK FROM THE HOLY LAND.

I KNOW THEIR STYLE WELL ENOUGH. YOU RECALL WE SAW KING RICHARD HIMSELF LEAD OFF HIS CRUSADING ARMY, WILL?
IF YOU INSIST ON GOING, LITTLE JOHN AND I WILL KEEP WATCH FROM THE CROWD.

THE DAY OF THE FAIR SOON ARRIVES...
STEP UP AND SEE THE LATEST WONDERS FROM THE HOLY LAND!
♪ I LOVED A MAIDEN FAIR OF FACE, HER THOUGHTS AND DEEDS WERE BOUND BY GRACE... ♪

TRINKETS AND NOVELTIES!
PASS AN HOUR WITH OUR **STROLLING PLAYERS!**

THE HIGHLIGHT OF THE DAY IS THE ARCHERY CONTEST.
HURRAH!
THWACK!
WHOOOSH!
HUNDREDS OF COMPETITORS ARE WHITTLED DOWN, UNTIL...
THREE CHALLENGERS REMAIN.
MASTER JAMES FORESTER FROM NORFOLK...
HURRAH!
THOMAS SNIPE, A CAPTAIN IN THE SHERIFF'S GUARD...
BOO!
AND A VETERAN CRUSADER.
HOORAY!
WHOEVER SHOOTS CLOSEST TO THE MIDDLE OF THE TARGET SHALL CLAIM THE PRIZE.

FORESTER IS THE FIRST TO SHOOT...
WHOOOSH!
THUD!
HURRAH!

I FANCY I CAN **BETTER THAT,** PEASANT!
WHOOOSH!
THWACK!
A BULLS EYE!

IT SEEMS SNIPE'S SHOT IS UNBEATABLE, BUT THEN...
CRACK!
WHOOOSH!
HE'S **SPLIT** SNIPE'S ARROW!
NOT **BAD,** CAPTAIN. BUT THE CONTEST'S **NOT OVER** YET.

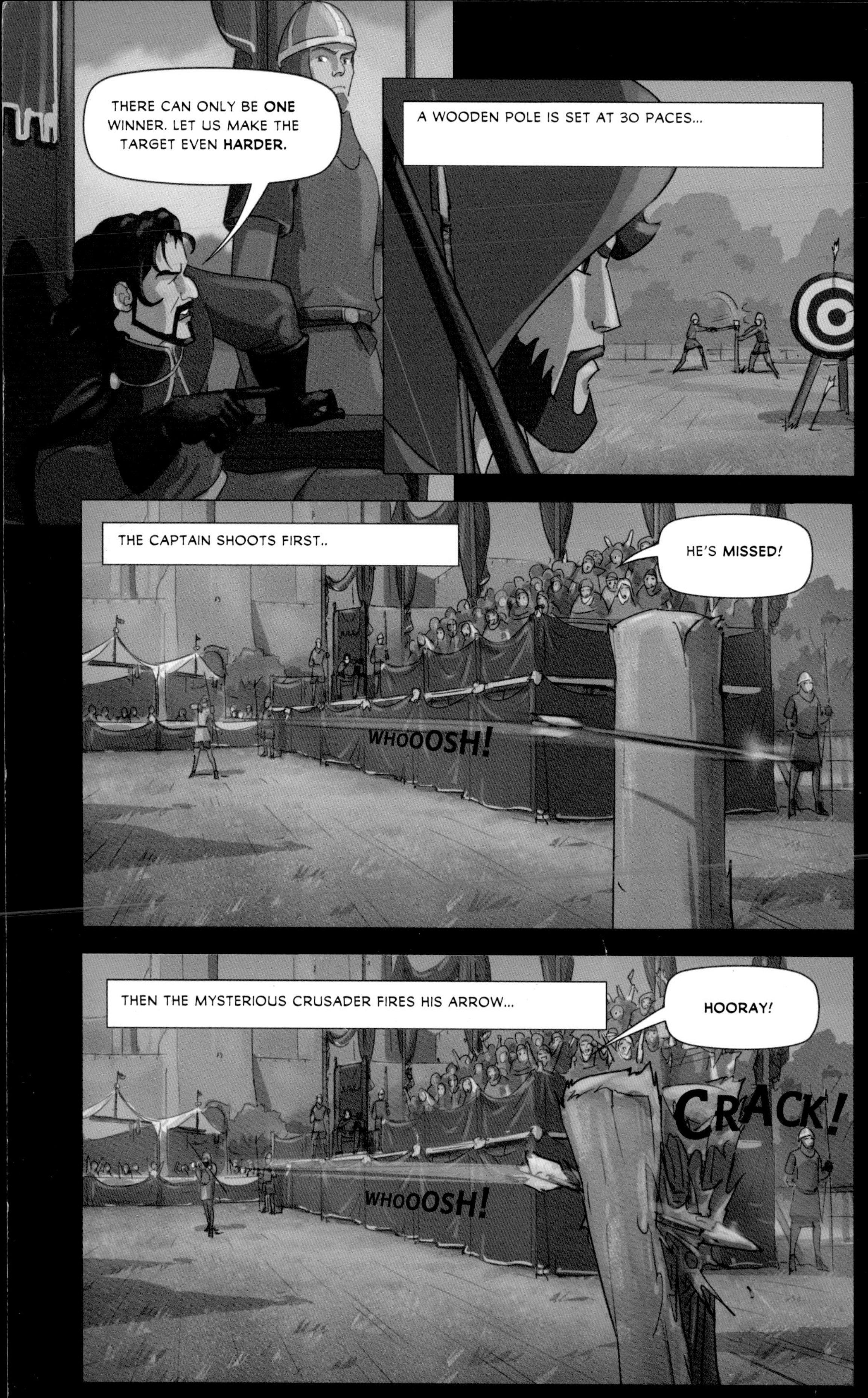
THERE CAN ONLY BE **ONE** WINNER. LET US MAKE THE TARGET EVEN **HARDER.**
A WOODEN POLE IS SET AT 30 PACES...
THE CAPTAIN SHOOTS FIRST..
HE'S **MISSED!**
WHOOOSH!
THEN THE MYSTERIOUS CRUSADER FIRES HIS ARROW...
HOORAY!
CRACK!
WHOOOSH!

I CLAIM MY PRIZE, SHERIFF.
YOU SHALL GET WHAT YOU DESERVE...
NOW!
YOU WALKED RIGHT INTO MY TRAP, ROBIN HOOD.
SEIZE HIM!
WHHAAAAA!

WILL AND LITTLE JOHN CAN ONLY WATCH IN HORROR, AS ROBIN IS OVERPOWERED...
I TOLD HIM IT WAS TOO RISKY!
SHALL WE TACKLE THE GUARDS?
THERE ARE TOO MANY OF THEM.
TAKE HIM TO THE HIGH TOWER!
LET'S GET BACK TO SHERWOOD AND TELL THE OTHERS.
SEE WHAT HAPPENS TO THE ENEMIES OF PRINCE JOHN!

ROBIN SOON FINDS HIMSELF A PRISONER IN NOTTINGHAM CASTLE, FORCED TO LISTEN TO THE SHERIFF'S MOCKING WORDS...
HA HA! SO MUCH FOR THE INVINCIBLE ROBIN HOOD!
NO CASTLE CAN HOLD ME FOR LONG.
YOU WON'T HAVE TIME TO ESCAPE.
BUT DON'T WORRY. I'LL MAKE SURE YOU STILL RECEIVE YOUR SILVER ARROW...
STRAIGHT THROUGH THE HEART AT NOON TOMORROW!

ROBIN SPENDS A SLEEPLESS NIGHT. THEN, AS DAWN BREAKS...
A HUNTING HORN, AT THIS HOUR?
TARRA!
NEXT MOMENT...
WHOOOSHH!
WHAT IN HEAVEN'S NAME...?
IT SEEMS ALL IS NOT LOST, AFTER ALL.
GOOD OLD LITTLE JOHN!

OOF!
WHA..?
HOOD'S ESCAPING!

WHOOSHH!
WHOOSHH!
WHOOSHH!
ONLY A FEW FEET TO GO...

I OWE YOU MY LIFE, LITTLE JOHN!
HURRY NOW...
...YOU CAN THANK MARIAN LATER. IT WAS HER IDEA.

WHOOSHH!
WHOOSHH!
MAKE HASTE! BEFORE WE ALL END UP AT THE SHERIFF'S MERCY.

THE SHERIFF'S MEN ARE SOON IN HOT PURSUIT...

THE TRIO PUSH THEIR MOUNTS TO THE LIMIT, BUT...
THEY'RE GAINING ON US!
HEAD FOR THE RIVER!
NOW WHAT?
TIME TO SAY GOODBYE TO YOUR MOUNT...

SLAP!
THAT'LL GIVE THEM A TRAIL TO FOLLOW.
BY THE TIME THE SHERIFF'S MEN REALIZE THEY'VE BEEN TRICKED, ROBIN AND HIS FRIENDS HAVE PUT ENOUGH DISTANCE BETWEEN THEM TO EVADE CAPTURE...
ALAN-A-DALE LIVES NEARBY. HE'LL HIDE US 'TIL NIGHTFALL.

TETHERING THEIR HORSES BY THE STREAM, ROBIN AND HIS FRIENDS WALK TO ALAN'S COTTAGE...
ROBIN OLD FRIEND! WHAT BRINGS YOU HERE?
WHEN ROBIN HAS TOLD ALAN AND HIS WIFE HIS STORY...
YOU'RE WELCOME TO HIDE HERE FOR AS LONG AS YOU LIKE.
THANKS. WE'LL RETURN TO SHERWOOD AS SOON AS IT'S DARK.
ROBIN AND HIS FRIENDS SPEND AN ANXIOUS DAY IN HIDING. AS DARKNESS FALLS...
FETCH THE TWO HORSES, FROM THE STREAM, LITTLE JOHN.
I'LL LEND YOU MY MARE AS WELL.
THANK YOU.

MINUTES LATER, LITTLE JOHN RETURNS...

BUT WHILE HE TAKES THE HORSES TO THE YARD AT THE REAR...
CRUNCH!
WHAT WAS THAT **NOISE** OUTSIDE?

LITTLE JOHN?
NO. IT CAME FROM THE **FRONT** OF THE COTTAGE.

LITTLE JOHN MUST HAVE BEEN **FOLLOWED.**

THE NEXT MOMENT...
THUD!
THUD!
THUD!

GIVE YOURSELF UP, LOCKSLEY! WE HAVE YOU TRAPPED.
BARRICADE THE DOOR!

SMASH!
WHOOSHH!
WHOOSHH!
WHOOSHH!
GRAB YOUR WEAPONS!
THUD!
ARRGH!

THEN...
WHAT'S THAT SMELL?
BURNING!
THEY MUST HAVE SET FIRE TO THE ROOF!
YOU TWO TRY AND GET AWAY WITH ALAN AND HIS WIFE.
I'LL KEEP GISBOURNE BUSY.
BUT ROBIN...
JUST GO!
COME OUT AND SURRENDER, LOCKSLEY!

I'M NOT DONE YET, GISBOURNE!
AN ARROW WHIZZES PAST ROBIN'S CHEEK...
THAT WAS CLOSE!
WHOOSHH!
WITH SMOKE CHOKING HIS LUNGS, ROBIN IS FORCED TO RETREAT...
COUGH! I THOUGHT I TOLD YOU TO...
I KNOCKED OUT THOSE SOLDIERS SO MARIAN AND THE OTHERS COULD GET AWAY. LET'S JOIN THEM!

JUST THEN, THE THATCH ERUPTS INTO FLAME...
NEEEIGH!
WHOOMPF!

LITTLE JOHN'S HORSE BOLTS IN FRIGHT...
WOOOAH!
SECONDS LATER, GUY'S SOLDIERS SURROUND THE YARD...
YOU'RE TRAPPED LOCKSLEY. SURRENDER OR DIE!

SUDDENLY, A FIGURE APPEARS THROUGH THE SMOKE...
WHO ON EARTH...?
STAND FIRM, YOU FOOLS!
THE SMOKE CAUSES ROBIN TO PASS OUT, BUT THE MYSTERIOUS KNIGHT CARRIES HIM AWAY TO SAFETY...

THE NEXT MORNING, ROBIN AWAKES IN A CLEARING IN SHERWOOD...
IT SEEMS I OWE MY LIFE TO THAT MYSTERIOUS KNIGHT.
I WONDER WHAT BECAME OF HIM?
ROBIN RETURNS TO HIS CAMP AND RECOUNTS HIS ESCAPE...
THANK HEAVENS YOU'RE SAFE.
WE NEED YOU MORE THAN EVER!
EARLY THIS MORNING, TWO OF OUR MEN WERE CAUGHT BY GISBOURNE OUTSIDE THE FOREST.
ONE ESCAPED AFTER THE OTHER HAD BEEN FORCED TO REVEAL OUR LOCATION.
THEN WE MUST PREPARE TO FIGHT!

THE CAMP BECOMES A HIVE OF ACTIVITY...
STRETCH THE ROPE AS TIGHT AS YOU CAN!
HOIST THOSE NETS ALOFT!
TAKE CARE WITH THOSE GRAPPLING HOOKS.

DIG FASTER. WE HAVEN'T MUCH TIME.
I WANT OUR BEST BOWMEN UP IN THE TREES.
JUST BEFORE NOON...
THEY'RE COMING! A HUNDRED HORSEMEN AT LEAST.

GUY'S MEN SURGE TOWARDS THE CAMP...
ATTACK!
TAKE NO PRISONERS!
BUT ROBIN AND HIS OUTLAWS ARE READY...
WAAAAH!
AGGGH!

WHAT?!
HELP!
AGGGH!
WHIZZZZ!
WHIZZZZ!
URGGH!
WOOAH!

SOON GISBOURNE'S MEN ARE IN DISARRAY...
RETREAT!
HURRAH!
HA HA!
LOOK AT THEM GO!
WE'VE WON THE FIRST BATTLE.
BUT GISBOURNE AND HIS MEN WILL BE BACK.
THE NEXT TIME WE SHAN'T HAVE SURPRISE ON OUR SIDE.

A FEW HOURS LATER, ROBIN IS PROVED CORRECT...
THEY'RE BACK! ON FOOT THIS TIME, EXCEPT GISBOURNE.
JUST AS I FEARED.
TO ARMS!

FIRE!
WHIZzzz!
WHIZzzz!
WHIZzzz!

THIS TIME THE ENEMY ARE EQUIPPED TO RETALIATE...
AGGGH!
URRGH!
WHOOSHH!
CLASH!

CLANG!

THWACK!
GISBOURNE'S SOLDIERS FORCE THE OUTLAWS BACK INTO THE HEART OF THE FOREST...
ARRRRR!
YAAAAH!
GRAAAH!
RUN!

THE OUTLAWS FALL BACK, ONLY TO FIND THEIR WAY BLOCKED BY MORE OF GISBOURNE'S MEN...
WE HAVE THEM NOW!
START THE FIRES!
LET'S SEE YOU ESCAPE FROM THIS, LOCKSLEY!

THE OUTLAWS LOOK BEATEN, WHEN SUDDENLY FROM OUT OF NOWHERE...
THE BLACK KNIGHT!

THE MYSTERIOUS WARRIOR CHARGES AT GISBOURNE'S MEN....
WAH!
HOLD THE LINE, YOU FOOLS!
AGGH!

BUT GISBOURNE'S MEN RECALL THE KNIGHT FROM THE PREVIOUS EVENING...
HE WALKED THROUGH FIRE!
RUN FOR YOUR LIVES!
HE'S NOT HUMAN!
WHILE GISBOURNE'S MEN PANIC, THE OUTLAWS TAKE CONTROL...
PUT OUT THE FIRES!
REGROUP!

PUSH GISBOURNE'S MEN TOWARDS THE RIVER!
YAAAH!
RETREAT!
WHAT'S YOUR PLAN, ROBIN?
IF WE CAN FORCE THEM INTO THE MARSHES, WE HAVE A CHANCE.

YOU BOWMEN, KEEP TO THE DRY GROUND! EVERYONE ELSE, FORWARD...
...BUT MAKE SURE YOU STAY IN SHALLOW WATER.
THE OUTLAWS DRIVE THEIR ENEMIES INTO THE MISTY MARSHES...
ARRRRR!
CLASH!
YAAAAH!

AGGH!
CLANG!
GRAAAH!

GISBOURNE'S MEN SOON FIND THEMSELVES SLOWED DOWN BY THE BOGGY GROUND...
SQUELCH!
...A SITTING TARGET FOR ROBIN'S ARCHERS...
URGH!
WHOOSHH!
WHOOSHH!
AAGH!

NEEEIGH!
WAH!
COME BACK, YOU COWARDS!
THE REMAINING SOLDIERS MANAGE TO GET FREE AND REACH THE OTHER SIDE OF THE MARSHES...
WE HAVE GISBOURNE NOW!
LEAVE HIM TO ME. WE HAVE A SCORE TO SETTLE.

YOU MAY HAVE WON THE **BATTLE** LOCKSLEY...
...BUT YOU **WON'T** LEAVE THE FIELD **ALIVE!**
WE'LL **SEE** ABOUT THAT!
CLANG!

RRAAAAH!
CLASH!
URGH!
ARGH!

YOU'RE **DONE FOR,** THIS TIME, LOCKSLEY!
'GASP'... NOT... QUITE...
URGH!
THRUST!

IT'S **OVER!**
WELL DONE, ROBIN!

WE DIDN'T DO IT ALL BY OURSELVES, REMEMBER.

OUR **MYSTERIOUS PROTECTOR** WAS THERE WHEN WE NEEDED HIM.
WHO **ARE** YOU SIR?

YOUR MAJESTY!
IT'S KING RICHARD HIMSELF!
WORD OF YOUR DEEDS REACHED ME IN THE HOLY LANDS, MASTER LOCKSLEY.

WHEN ROBIN HAS TOLD THE KING HIS TALE...
FEAR NOT, MASTER LOCKSLEY. YOUR LANDS WILL BE RETURNED TO YOU.
THANK YOU, YOUR MAJESTY.
AND ANY OF YOUR MEN WHO WISH TO ENTER MY SERVICE WILL BE WELCOME.
THREE CHEERS FOR THE KING!
NOW YOUR MAJESTY HAS RETURNED, I MUST BE TRUE TO MY WORD...
FRIAR TUCK - YOU HAVE A WEDDING TO PERFORM!

WITH LITTLE JOHN AS HIS BEST MAN, ROBIN'S MARRIAGE TO MARIAN IS FINALLY COMPLETED...
...YOU MAY KISS THE BRIDE.
CONGRATULATIONS TO YOU BOTH.
HOORAY!
NOW WE CAN CELEBRATE!
I FEAR THE CELEBRATIONS MUST WAIT. OUR LANDS ARE NOT YET FREE.
BUT ROBIN...

ALAS, YOUR LEADER IS **RIGHT.**
I HAVE A **SCORE** TO SETTLE WITH THE SHERIFF, NOT TO MENTION MY **DEVIOUS** BROTHER, JOHN.
I WILL NEED **EVERY** LOYAL SUBJECT **ALONGSIDE** ME.
AND SO, LED BY THEIR KING, ROBIN HOOD AND HIS BAND OF BRAVE OUTLAWS SET OFF FOR NOTTINGHAM AND MORE EXCITING ADVENTURES...
THE END

The story of Robin Hood

The daring, adventurous figure of Robin Hood has enthralled and entertained people of all ages for over 600 years. But where did his story begin, and did such a man really exist?

Medieval minstrels

The earliest known reference to the character is in an English poem called *Piers Plowman* written in the late 14th century. But Robin Hood truly comes into his own in the English ballads of the late 15th and early 16th centuries. Ballads were stories designed to be sung, and were made popular by wandering minstrels who performed them at inns, markets and noblemen's halls.

The earliest surviving ballad referring to Robin Hood is called *Robin and the Monk,* and it features the city of Nottingham as well as Robin's rivalry with the Sheriff.

Alongside Robin and the Sheriff of Nottingham, Guy of Gisbourne, Little John, Much and Will Scarlet all make their first appearances in these early ballads. Maid Marian and Friar Tuck weren't introduced until later.

Robin is described as a yeoman, which was somewhere between a peasant and a knight in status. It wasn't until two plays written in the late 16th century that he was presented as a former nobleman, with the title Earl of Huntingdon. Also around that time came the first mention of Robin robbing from the rich to give to the poor.

From the days of the early ballads, Robin Hood has been associated with two different regions: Sherwood Forest in Nottinghamshire and Barnsdale in Yorkshire.

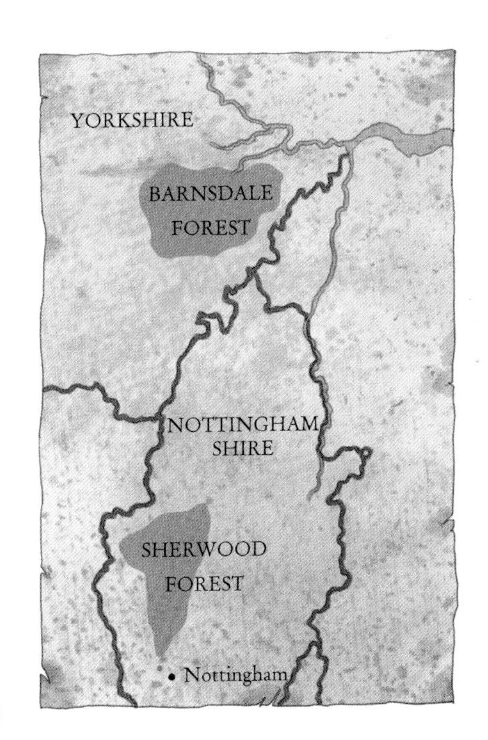

Barnsdale and Sherwood

Robin and the Monk features Sherwood Forest, while another early ballad, *A Gest of Robyn Hode,* mentions both Nottingham and Barnsdale.

It is written in a style closer to that of Yorkshire than Nottinghamshire. Some people have argued that this suggests the tales originated in the northern county.

However, Barnsdale is only one day's ride from the north of Sherwood Forest, so it's possible that one band of outlaws could have been active in both areas.

May Day games

The legend of Robin Hood also became popular through games that were played as part of medieval May Day festivals. During these games, festivalgoers would dress up as Robin or one of his associates.

A Gest of Robyn Hode is one of the earliest existing printed versions of the legend. After printing became widespread in the late 15th century, Robin appeared in something called a broadside ballad. A broadside was a single sheet of cheap paper printed on one side with a ballad, rhyme or news, often decorated with woodcut illustrations.

Alan-a-Dale first appeared in one such broadside ballad in the 17th century. The ballads were later collected into garlands, a name for cheaply printed books designed to be bought by the poor.

Robin Hood was also mentioned by the playwright William Shakespeare in several of his plays, including *The Two Gentlemen of Verona* and *As You Like It.*

In 1795, the writer Joseph Ritson published a collection of ballads which included a biography of Robin Hood. According to Ritson, Robin Hood was born around 1160 in the Nottinghamshire village of Locksley, and his real name was Robert Fitzooth.

In 1883, American author Robert Pyle wrote *The Merry Adventures of Robin Hood*, one of the first retellings aimed specifically at children. Many subsequent adaptations of the legend took inspiration from this version.

With the invention of radio, film and television, Robin Hood was brought to new generations. *The Adventures of Robin Hood* (1938) and *Robin Hood: Prince of Thieves* (1991) are two of the most famous movie versions of the legend. His best-known appearances on television include *The Adventures of Robin Hood* (1955-59), *Robin of Sherwood* (1984-86) and *Robin Hood* (2006-09).

Some experts believe that although Robin Hood is now largely known as a fictional character, the stories are based on a real person. But exactly who that person was will probably never be discovered. Variations on the name Robin Hood were fairly common in medieval England. From 1261 onwards it appears on several lists of criminals across England, from Berkshire in the south to Yorkshire in the north.

Robin Hood may have even been a standard alias used by thieves. So if the famous outlaw did exist, his real name will almost certainly remain unknown.

But whether he was a real person or not, the name of Robin Hood has become so well-loved all over the world that the man and his adventures will never die.

Robin Hood

Russell Punter was born in Bedfordshire, England. From an early age he enjoyed writing and illustrating his own stories. He trained as a graphic designer at art college in West Sussex before entering publishing in 1987. He has written over fifty books for children, ranging from original rhyming stories to adaptations of classic novels.

Matteo Pincelli was born in Bergamo, Italy. He studied anatomy and comics drawing in Bologna and later formed an animation studio together with eight colleagues. He has also worked in France with a production company based in Paris, and has lived in Berlin, Germany, and Milan, Italy. Today he is based in Fano in the Marche region of Italy, where he occupies himself mainly with work as a storyboard artist, television cartoonist and illustrator of children's books.

Mike Collins has been creating comics for over 25 years. Starting on *Spider-Man* and *Transformers* for Marvel UK, he has also worked for DC, 2000AD and a host of other publishers. In that time he's written or drawn almost all the major characters for each company – *Wonder Woman, Batman, Superman, Flash, Teen Titans, X-Men, Captain Britain, Judge Dredd, Sláine, Rogue Trooper, Darkstars, Peter Cannon: Thunderbolt* and more. He currently draws a series of noir crime fiction graphic novels, *Varg Veum*, in Norse. He also provides storyboards for TV and films, including *Doctor Who, Sherlock, Igam Ogam, Claude, Hana's Helpline* and *Horrid Henry*.

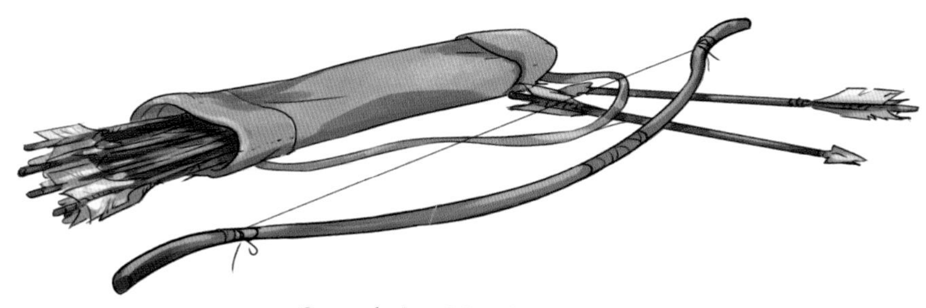

Cover design: Matt Preston

First published in 2017 by Usborne Publishing Ltd., Usborne House, 83-85 Saffron Hill, London EC1N 8RT, England. www.usborne.com